P9-DDV-593

Great news for anyone who has ever purred over the best-selling The Cat Who ... mysteries! Fictional columnist James Qwilleran has finally completed his book showcasing the stories related to him by residents of Moose County—that famous region four hundred miles north of everywhere. As devoted readers of the cat capers know, Qwill has been working on this book since *The Cat Who Tailed a Thief*. Now he has compiled all the stories in *Short & Tall Tales*.

Lilian Jackson Braun introduces the prize-winning reporter and recounts how he collected these captivating tales, while Qwill himself has written a preface for each that provides insight about the storyteller and the circumstances. Revealing the offbeat "history" of Moose County, this delightful volume is a treat for old and new fans alike.

Praise for The Cat Who ... novels:

"Her storytelling voice ... is filled with enough sense of wonder and whimsy to turn her yarns into ideal bedtime tales for grown-ups."   —*Los Angeles Times*

"The feelings produced by reading about Qwill and his pals can best be compared to that coziest of feelings—having a purring cat on your lap."   —*Booklist*

TITLES BY LILIAN JACKSON BRAUN

▼▼▼

SHORT STORY COLLECTIONS

Short *and* Tall Tales

Moose County Legends Collected by
James Mackintosh Qwilleran

Lilian Jackson Braun

JOVE BOOKS, NEW YORK

This is a work of fiction. Names, characters, places, and incidents either are the product of the author's imagination or are used fictitiously, and any resemblance to actual persons, living or dead, business establishments, events, or locales is entirely coincidental.

SHORT & TALL TALES

A Jove Book / published by arrangement with
the author

PRINTING HISTORY
G. P. Putnam's Sons hardcover edition / October 2002
Jove edition / December 2003

Copyright © 2002 by Lilian Jackson Braun
Cover art by Teresa Fasolino
Cover design by Walter Harper

Interior illustrations courtesy of Dover Publications, Inc.:
Advertising Spot Illustrations of the Twenties and Thirties;
Humorous Victorian Spot Illustrations; 3,800 Old-Time Fashioned
Cuts; 3,800 Early Advertising Cuts; and *Victorian Goods and*
Merchandise, 2,300 Illustrations.

Substantial portions of this work have appeared in
prior books in The Cat Who . . . series.

For information address: The Berkley Publishing Group,
a division of Penguin Group (USA) Inc.,
375 Hudson Street, New York, New York 10014.

ISBN: 0-515-13635-2

A JOVE BOOK®
Jove Books are published by The Berkley Publishing Group,
a division of Penguin Group (USA) Inc.,
375 Hudson Street, New York, New York 10014.
JOVE and the "J" design
are trademarks belonging to Penguin Group (USA) Inc.

PRINTED IN THE UNITED STATES OF AMERICA

10 9 8 7 6 5 4 3 2 1

Dedicated to Earl Bettinger,
The Husband Who . . .

JAMES MACKINTOSH QWILLERAN
WISHES TO SAY:

"Let us give credit where credit is least expected. To the automated coffeemaker that did yeoman duty during the preparation of this book. To my trusty typing machine, older than I am and still clicking. To Kao K'o Kung and Yum Yum, who sat tirelessly on my desk, supervising. Koko, as he is known, was ever willing to stare at my forehead when I was slow in thinking of the right word. Yum Yum, my official Muse, inspired with her mere presence and never once caught her whiskers in the typewriter platen."

Contents .

▼▼▼

▼▼▼

Short *and*
Tall Tales

Introduction

by Lilian Jackson Braun

When James Mackintosh Qwilleran and his tape recorder left the crowding and anonymity of the megalopolis and discovered Moose County, 400 miles north of everywhere, he learned two things: In a small rural community, everyone is a celebrity, and everyone has a story to tell.

Here was a journalist who had never known his grandparents or even his own father! And he was interviewing folks whose roots went back to 1850. Their tales were short, and some were beyond belief. He listened and captured them for this volume of *Short and Tall Tales*. Also included are some

▼▼▼

1

of Qwilleran's own research papers based on chats with historians, members of the Oldtimers Club (no one under eighty), and descendants of backwoods pioneers.

A word about the author: Qwill, as he likes to be called, was a prize-winning journalist on major newspapers Down Below—until circumstances (read "an inheritance") caused him to go native, so to speak. He is a tall, rugged individual, if middle aged, with graying hair, an oversize mustache that is much admired, and brooding eyes that harbor both sympathy and a sense of humor. He lives in a converted barn in Pickax City, the county seat (population 3,000). As is well known, his housemates are two Siamese cats. And yes, he has a girlfriend.

1.

The Legend of
the Rubbish Heap

A Chronicle of Two Pioneer Families

How a miraculous bit of good luck started a three-generation course of success and disappointment, love and hatred, disaster and . . . all's well that ends well. It happened in Moose County, and details are corroborated by interviews with oldtimers and by diaries, letters, and other documents in the Pickax historical collection.

—JMQ

In the mid–nineteenth century, when Moose County was beginning to boom, it was a Gold Rush without the gold. There were veins of coal to be mined, forests to be lumbered, granite to be quarried, land to be developed, fortunes to be made. It would become the richest county in the state.

In 1859 two penniless youths from Germany arrived by schooner, by way of Canada. On setting foot on the foreign soil, they looked this way and that to get their bearings, and both saw it at the same time! A piece of paper money in a rubbish heap! Without stopping to inquire its value, they tore it in half to signify their partnership. It would be share and share alike from then on.

Their names were Otto Wilhelm Limburger and Karl Gustav Klingenschoen. They were fifteen years old.

Labor was needed. They hired on as carpenters, worked long hours, obeyed orders, learned everything they could, used their wits, watched for opportunities, took chances, borrowed wisely, cheated a little, and finally launched a venture of their own.

By the time they were in their thirties, Otto and Karl dominated the food and shelter industry. They owned all the rooming houses, eating places, and travelers' inns along the shoreline. Only then did they marry: Otto, a God-fearing woman named Gretchen; Karl, a fun-loving woman nicknamed Minnie. At the double wedding the friends pledged to name their children after each other. They hoped for boys, but girls could be named Karla and Wilhelmina. Thus the two families became even more entwined . . . until rumors about Karl's wife started drifting back

▼▼▼

from the waterfront. When Karl denied the slander, Otto trusted him.

But there was more! One day Karl approached his partner with an idea for expanding their empire. They would add saloons, dance halls, and female entertainment of various kinds. Otto was outraged! The two men argued. They traded insults. They even traded a few blows and, with noses bleeding, tore up the fragments of currency that had been in their pockets since the miracle of the rubbish heap.

Karl proceeded on his own and did extremely well, financially. To prove it, he built a fine fieldstone mansion in Pickax City, across from the courthouse. In retaliation Otto imported masons and woodworkers from Europe to build a brick palace in the town of Black Creek. How the community reacted to the two architectural wonders should be mentioned. The elite of the county vied for invitations to sip tea and view Otto's black walnut woodwork; Karl and Minnie sent out invitations to a party and no one came.

When it was known that the brick mansion

would be the scene of a wedding, the best families could talk of nothing else. The bride was Otto's only daughter; he had arranged for her to marry a suitable young man from the Goodwinter family; the date was set. Who would be invited? Was it true that Otto had taken his daughter before a magistrate and legally changed her name from Karla to Elsa? It was true. Elsa's dower chest was filled with fine household linens and intimate wedding finery. Gifts were being delivered in the best carriages in town. Seamstresses were working overtime on costumes for the wedding guests. Gowns for the bridal party were being shipped from Germany. Suppose there was a storm at sea! Suppose they did not arrive in time!

Then, on the very eve of the nuptials, Otto's daughter eloped with the youngest son of Karl Klingenschoen!

Shock, embarrassment, sheer horror, and the maddening suspicion that Karl and Minnie had promoted the defection—all these emotions combined to affect Otto's mind.

As for the young couple, there were rumors that they had gone to San Francisco. When the news came, a few years later, that the young couple had lost their lives in the earthquake, Elsa's father had no idea who they were.

Karl and Minnie lived out their lives in the most splendid house in Pickax, ignored by everyone of social standing. Karl never knew that his immense fortune was wiped out, following the financial crash of 1929.

Toward the end of the century, Otto's sole descendant was an eccentric who sat on the porch of the brick palace and threw stones at dogs.

Karl's sole descendant was Fanny Klingenschoen, who recovered her grandfather's wealth ten times over.

Eventually the saga of the two families took a curious twist. The Klingenschoen Foundation has purchased two properties from the Limburger estate: the mansion in Black Creek and the hotel in Pickax. The former has become the Nutcracker Inn; the latter is now the Mackintosh Inn. The "legend of the rubbish heap" has come full circle.

2.

Secret of the Blacksmith's Wife

Revealed to Her Grandson on Her Deathbed

Eddington Smith never revealed his grandmother's secret until he, too, was at death's door. Then he shared it with the local historian, and—as they say— one thing led to another. The secret has outlived the statute of limitations.

—JMQ

When Pickax was named the county seat—because of its central location—it was only a hamlet, but a building boom started almost overnight. The blacksmith, who made nails as well as horseshoes, could hardly keep up with the demand as ambitious settlers built dwellings and shops. Then one day he was kicked in the head by a horse and died on the spot. There was panic in Pickax! No blacksmith! No nails!

The next day, by a strange coincidence, a stranger walked into town—a big brawny man carrying a stick over his shoulder with a bundle tied on the end. He wore his hair longer than was

▼▼▼

the custom in Moose County, and at first he was viewed with suspicion. When he said he was a blacksmith, however, the townfolk changed their attitude.

Could he make nails?

Yes, he could make nails.

What was his name?

John.

John what?

He said, "Just John. That's all the name you need to make nails."

This was somewhat irregular, but they needed nails, so the local officials put their heads together and listed him on the town rolls as John B. Smith, the middle initial standing for "Black".

When Longfellow wrote "The smith a mighty man is he," he might have been writing about John B. He was tall and broad-shouldered, with *large and sinewy hands*, and his muscles were *strong as iron bands*. No one dared criticize his long hair. Furthermore, he was twenty-two and good-looking, and all the young women in town were after him. It was not long before he married Emma, who could read and write. They had six

▼▼▼

children, although only three reached adult-hood—not an unusual situation in those days. He built them a house of quarry stone with a front of feldspar that sparkled like diamonds on a sunny day. It was much admired by the other settlers, who liked novelty.

The smithy was in the backyard, and there John worked industriously, turning out tools, wagon wheels, cookpots, horseshoes, and nails. He was a good provider and went to chapel with his family twice a week. Emma was the envy of most women in town.

Once in a while he told her he had to visit his old mother in Lockmaster, and he would get on his horse and ride south, staying a week or more. The local gossips said he had another wife down there, but Emma trusted him, and he always brought her a pretty shawl or a nice piece of cloth to make into a dress.

Then came a time when he failed to return. There was no way of tracing his whereabouts, but Emma was sure he had been killed by highway-men who wanted to steal his horse and gold watch. Lockmaster—with its fur-trading and gold-

▼▼▼

mining—offered rich pickings for robbers. Someone from the next town wanted to buy John's anvil
and tools, but Emma refused to sell.

Yet as time went on and she thought about his
past behavior, she remembered how he used to go
out into the yard in the middle of the night without a lantern. She never asked questions, and he
never explained, but she could hear the sound of
digging. That was not so unusual; there were no
banks, and valuables were often buried. Then she
recalled that it always happened after a visit to his
old mother.

Emma was fired by curiosity, and she went out
to the smithy with a shovel. It was dark, but she
went without a lantern rather than arouse further
gossip. Most of the yard was trampled hard as a
rock. There was one spot near the big tree where
she tried digging. There were tree roots. She found
another spot.

Then, just as she was about to give up, her
shovel struck metal. She dropped to her knees and
began scraping the soil furiously with her bare
hands, gradually exposing an iron chest. With her
hands trembling and heart pounding, she opened

▼▼▼

the lid. The chest was filled with gold coins! Frightened by the sight, she closed the lid and knelt there, hugging her arms in thought—deep thought. There had been a dark rag on top of the gold. Once more she opened the lid—just a few inches—and reached in stealthily as if afraid to touch the coins. Pulling out the rag, she took it indoors to examine by lamplight.

It was bright red. It was the red bandanna that a pirate tied around his head.

She went back to the yard, covered the chest with soil, stamping it down with her feet. The next day she had the yard paved with cobblestones.

Emma had always wondered where her husband had acquired his gold watch.

▼▼▼

3.

Housecalls on Horseback

A Look at the Medical Profession—
A Long Time Ago

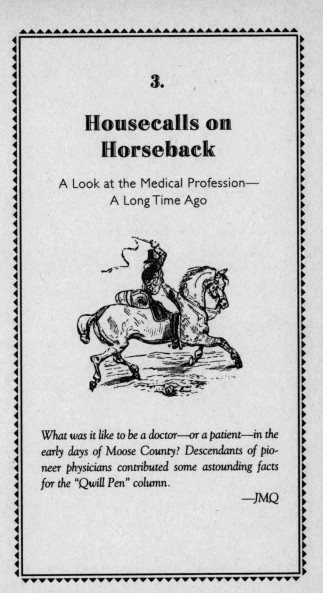

What was it like to be a doctor—or a patient—in the early days of Moose County? Descendants of pioneer physicians contributed some astounding facts for the "Qwill Pen" column.

—JMQ

A knock on the door in the middle of the night! A farmer standing on the doorstep.

"Doctor, come quick! My wife—she's got the fever! She's ravin' like a madwoman!"

No time to lose. Throw on some clothes. Saddle the horse. Grab the medical bag with the long shoulder strap. And off into the dark night at a gallop, to a crude log cabin in the woods.

Physicians were needed desperately in Moose County 150 years ago—not only to treat fevers, smallpox, and lung disease, but to rush to the scene of accidents. Pioneer life was filled with hazards. Widespread forest fires caused great suffering.

▼▼▼

Spring floods, poisonous snakes, runaway horses, kicking mules, hunting mishaps, shipwrecks, and mining accidents increased the casualty list. Moreover, a major industry—lumbering—was a dangerous one. Lumbermen were injured horribly in the woods, on the river during spring log drives, and around the sawmills that operated at the river's mouth. Amputations were a frequent necessity in the risky business of cutting, milling, and shipping lumber—not to mention the casual amputation of an ear in a saloon brawl on a Saturday night.

The local physician, if the community happened to have one, responded to calls for help day or night, in any weather. No wonder the pioneers referred to him as "the good doctor." In the spring he rode his horse through deep mud and swollen streams. In the summer he fought the mosquitoes that infested the swampland. In the winter he rode against biting winds from the lake and through blinding blizzards, sometimes a few yards ahead of a howling pack of wolves. Or he trudged cross-country on snowshoes and struggled through snowdrifts to reach the door of a remote cabin.

At the patient's bedside he administered the

▼▼▼

simple remedies carried in his knapsack. He might have to use crude material for bandages and make splints from whatever boards were at hand.

The pioneer doctor carried his drugstore in his shoulder bag or in the saddlebags on his horse. There were powders for colds and fevers and rheumatism. There were potions in corked bottles for use as tonics or as remedies for croup or snakebite. His miracle drugs were rhubarb powder, quinine flakes, digitalis, arnica, capsicum, nux vomica, and the like, many of which had been used in healing for centuries. The backwoods physician also carried a pair of "twisters" for pulling teeth.

He might put arnica lotion on a wound while fighting off the flies and perform surgery by candlelight in a cabin that was as dark in daytime as it was at night. Then he probably prescribed rest and a diet of gruel for the patient, before riding back to town on his horse. If it was still daylight, he let the horse find its way home while he himself rocked in the saddle and caught up with his reading of the latest medical journals.

For his labor the pioneer doctor was often paid

▼▼▼

in eggs and homemade butter, or a scrawny hen. Later, a patient might take a bushel of apples to the doctor's house or a piece of fresh pork when the pig was slaughtered. Another would offer to plow his field or chop a cord of wood in return for medical care.

Why did these physicians brave the wilderness a hundred years ago? Many were young men with the ink barely dry on their diplomas. They came from medical schools in Detroit, Toronto, Cincinnati, and Louisville, sailing up the lake in a schooner that was destined to pick up a load of lumber. Pioneering was the spirit of the times, and the wilderness was an adventure for young doctors, as well as an opportunity to use their new skills and knowledge. No doubt they were gratified, also, by the instant acclaim and hospitality accorded a new physician in a frontier town. His presence relieved some of the terror of pioneer life.

Not every medical adventurer was willing to tolerate the hardships. He left after a year or two, and another fresh graduate took his place, arriving from the metropolis in a frock coat and top hat, befitting the dignity of the profession. He soon ex-

▼▼▼

changed that garb for a rough cloak and frontier hat, with high boots and a stout stick for tramping through woods and bogs.

Some doctors elected to stay in Moose County. The population of the area was increasing, the lumbering towns were thriving, and roads progressed from muddy ruts to decent dirt. The physician now used a cart or a horse and buggy for house calls, and a sleigh in winter. Saddlebags were replaced by the modern badge of the profession: the little black bag, in which babies were said to be delivered.

The general practitioner's office was in his front parlor. Counting office hours and house calls, he worked a twelve-hour day—more if there was an emergency in the middle of the night. Yet his patients did not always take his advice—as in the case of vaccination for the dreaded smallpox. In some towns not a single student answered the school bell on V-Day. Families clung to their old remedies: goose-grease plasters, onion poultices, catnip tea, beefsteak broth, and the trusted bottle of whiskey reserved for medicinal purposes.

▼▼▼

4.

Hilda the Clipper

She Put Fear into the Male
Population of One Small Town

Brrr happens to be the coldest town in Moose County. Is it a coincidence that it also has the largest number of "characters"? Hotelkeeper Gary Pratt tells about Hilda, and I believe every word!

—JMQ

My grandfather used to tell about this eccentric old woman in Brrr who had everybody terrorized. This was about seventy years ago, you understand. She always walked around town with a pair of hedge clippers, pointing them at people and going *click-click* with the blades. Behind her back they laughed and called her Hilda the Clipper, but the same people were very nervous when she was around.

The thing of it was, nobody knew if she was just an oddball or was really smart enough to beat the system. In stores she picked up anything she wanted without paying a cent. She broke all the town ordinances and got away with it. Once in a while a cop or the sheriff would question her from a safe distance, and she said she was taking her hedge clippers to be sharpened. She didn't have a hedge. She lived in a tar-paper shack with a mangy dog. No electricity, no running water. My grandfather had a farmhouse across the road, and Hilda's shack was on his property. She lived there rent-free, brought water in a pail from his hand pump, and helped herself to firewood from his woodpile in winter.

One night, right after Halloween, the Reverend Mr. Wimsey from the church here was driving home from a prayer meeting at Squunk Corners. It was a cold night, and cars didn't have heaters then. His Model T didn't even have side curtains, so he was dressed warm. He was chugging along the country road, at probably twenty miles an hour, when he saw somebody in the darkness ahead, trudging down the middle of the dirt road and wearing a bathrobe and bedroom slippers. She was carrying hedge clippers.

Mr. Wimsey knew her well. She'd been a member of his flock until he suggested she quit bring-

▼▼▼

ing the clippers to services. Then she gave up going to church and was kind of hostile. Still, he couldn't leave her out there to catch her death of cold. Nowadays you'd just call the sheriff, but there were no car radios then, and no cell phones. So he pulled up and asked where she was going.

"To see my friend," she said in a gravelly voice.

"Would you like a ride, Hilda?"

She gave him a mean look and then said, "Seein' as how it's a cold night . . ." She climbed in the car and sat with the clippers on her lap and both hands on the handles.

Mr. Wimsey told Grandpa he gulped a couple of times and asked where her friend lived.

"Over yonder." She pointed across a cornfield.

"It's late to go visiting," he said. "Wouldn't you rather I should take you home?"

"I told you where I be wantin' to go," she shouted, as if he was deaf, and she gave the clippers a *click-click.*

"That's all right, Hilda. Do you know how to get there?"

"It's over yonder." She pointed to the left.

At the next road he turned left and drove for

▼▼▼

about a mile without seeing anything like a house. He asked what the house looked like.

"I'll know it when we get there!" *Click-click.*

"What road is it on? Do you know?"

"It don't have a name." *Click-click.*

"What's the name of your friend?"

"None o' yer business! Just take me there."

She was shivering, and he stopped the car and started taking off his coat. "Let me put my coat around you, Hilda."

"Don't you get fresh with me!" she shouted, pushing him away and going *click-click.*

Mr. Wimsey kept on driving and thinking what to do. He drove past a sheep pasture, a quarry, and dark farmhouses with barking dogs. The lights of Brrr glowed in the distance, but if he steered in that direction, she went into a snit and clicked the clippers angrily.

Finally he had an inspiration. "We're running out of fuel!" he said in an anxious voice. "We'll be stranded out here! We'll freeze to death! I have to go into town to buy some gasoline!"

It was the first time in his life, he told Grandpa, that he'd ever told a lie, and he prayed silently for forgiveness. He also prayed the trick would work. Hilda didn't object. Luckily she was getting drowsy, probably in the first stages of hypothermia. Mr. Wimsey found a country store and went in to use their crank telephone.

In two minutes a sheriff deputy drove up on a motorcycle. "Mr. Wimsey! You old rascal!" he said to the preacher. "We've been looking all over for the Clipper! Better talk fast, or I'll have to arrest you for kidnapping!"

What happened, you see: Hilda's dog had been howling for hours, and Grandpa called the sheriff.

Eventually Hilda was lodged in a foster home—for her own protection—and had to surrender her hedge clippers. The whole town breathed a lot easier. I asked my grandfather why they put up with her eccentricities for so long. He said, "Folks still had the pioneer philosophy: Shut up and make do!"

▼▼▼

5.

Milo the Potato Farmer

As Thornton Haggis Heard the Tale from His Grandfather

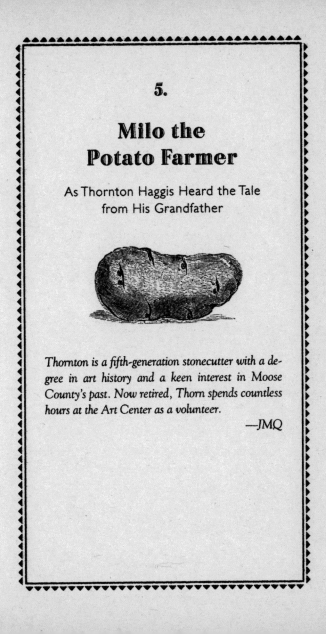

Thornton is a fifth-generation stonecutter with a degree in art history and a keen interest in Moose County's past. Now retired, Thorn spends countless hours at the Art Center as a volunteer.

—JMQ

Milo Thackeray and my grandfather were good friends. They played checkers and went hunting together—varmints and deer. Hunting was not a sport in those days. For many struggling families it was a way to put food on the table. Hard times had come to Moose County in the early twentieth century. Yet this had been the richest county in the state when natural resources were being exploited.

Then the ten mines closed, leaving entire villages without hope of work; the forests were lumbered out; there was no market for quarry stone; the ship-building industry went elsewhere when steamboats replaced tall-masted schooners. Thousands of persons fled Down Below, hoping to find work in factories, and those who remained had little money to spend on potatoes and tombstones. Milo was a potato farmer, and Gramps was a stonecutter.

It had been a year of tragedy for the potato farmer. His eldest son was one of the first casualties of World War One; two younger children died in the influenza epidemic; and now his wife died while giving birth to twins, Thelma and Thurston. They were his salvation! Gramps was there when Milo swore an oath to give them a better life than he had known. A sister-in-law came in to care for them, and eventually Milo married her. Eventually, too, his life took a strange turn.

In 1919 the Volstead Act went into effect, and thirsty citizens provided a large market for illegal beverages. Somehow, Milo learned he could make hard liquor from potatoes. Gramps helped him build a distillery, and it worked! Customers came to the farm in Model T cars and horse-drawn wagons. Unfortunately for the jubilant farmer, revenue agents also came. They smashed the still and poured the liquor on the ground. (Even to this day the belief persists that this act accounts for the superior flavor of Moose County potatoes.)

Milo was undaunted! His twins were growing fast, and he had sworn an oath.

Across the lake, a hundred miles away, was Canada, famous for good whiskey. On the shore of Moose County there were scores of commercial fishermen who were getting only a penny a pound for their catch. Milo organized a fleet of rumrunners to bring the whiskey over under cover of darkness. Soon a steady stream of Model T trucks was coming north to haul it away, camouflaged in many ingenious ways.

The poor potato farmer became the rich bootlegger.

Transactions were made in cash, and Gramps held the lantern while Milo buried the money in the backyard.

Every weekend Milo took his family and their young friends to Lockmaster for a picnic and moving picture show. The back of the truck was filled

▼▼▼

with kids sitting on disguised cases of contraband. Milo never attended the show, and the seats were never there for the return trip.

There was no such entertainment in Moose County. The twins begged their father to open a picture show in Pickax.

Prohibition ended in 1933, but the potato farmer was in a position to indulge his twins. He bought the old opera house, long boarded up, and made it the Pickax Movie Palace. He financed their chosen careers.

Besides their sex, the twins were very different. Thurston was slight of build and more sensitive; he loved dogs and horses and wanted to be a vet-erinarian. Milo sent him to Cornell, where he earned his DVM degree.

Thelma was taller, huskier, and bolder; she wanted to be "in pictures". Milo sent her to Holly-wood with her stepmother as chaperone. He never saw either of the women again.

Thelma obtained bit parts in two B films and decided she would prefer the food business, play-ing the leading role as hostess in her own restau-rant. Milo first financed a snack shop (the

▼▼▼

Thackeray Snackery) and then a fine restaurant called simply Thelma's. She did very well. When Milo died he left his fortune to Thurston, to establish the Thackeray Animal Clinic in Lockmaster, and to Thelma to realize her dream of a private dinner club for connoisseurs of old movies.

Milo was buried in the Hilltop Cemetery, with Gramps as the sole mourner. And Gramps chiseled the headstone the way his friend wanted it: MILO THE POTATO FARMER.

6.

The Little Old Man in the Woods

As Told by Dr. Bruce Abernethy,
Black Creek Pediatrician

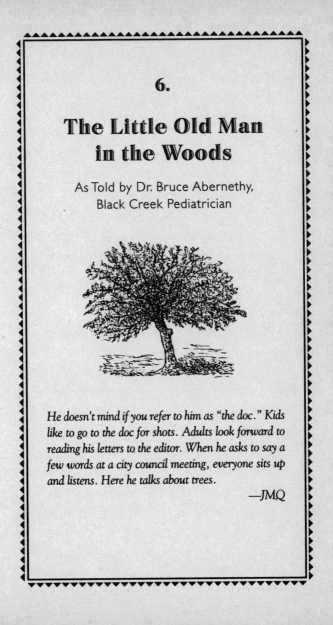

*He doesn't mind if you refer to him as "the doc." Kids
like to go to the doc for shots. Adults look forward to
reading his letters to the editor. When he asks to say a
few words at a city council meeting, everyone sits up
and listens. Here he talks about trees.*

—JMQ

When I was eleven years old, we were living in a wooded area outside Fishport, and behind our property was the forest primeval—or so I thought. It was a dense grove of trees that had a sense of mystery for an eleven-year-old. I used to go there to get away from my younger siblings and read about flying saucers. A certain giant tree with a spreading root system above ground provided comfortable seating in a kind of mossy hammock.

I would sneak off on a Saturday afternoon with the latest science fiction magazine—and a supply of pears. You see, the early French explorers had planted pear trees up and down the lakeshore. To

▼▼▼

own a "French pear tree" was a mark of distinction. We had one that was still bearing luscious fruit. Before leaving on my secret Saturday reading binge, I would climb up into the tree and stuff my shirtfront with pears. Then I'd slink away into the forest.

One day I was lounging between the huge roots of my favorite tree and reading in pop-eyed wonder about the mysteries of outer space, when I heard a rustling in the tree above me. I looked up, expecting a squirrel, and saw a pair of legs dangling from the mass of foliage: clunky brown shoes, woolly brown kneesocks, brown leather breeches. A moment later, a small man dropped to the ground—or rather floated to earth. He was old, with a flowing gray mustache, and he wore a pointed cap like a woodpecker's, with the brim pulled down over his eyes. Most amazingly, he was only about three feet tall.

I wanted to say something like: Hello . . . Who are you? . . . Where did you come from? But I was absolutely tongue-tied. Then he began to talk in a foreign language, and I had seen enough World War Two movies to know it was German.

▼▼▼

Now comes the strangest part: *I knew what he was saying!* His words were being interpreted by some kind of mental telepathy. He talked—in a kindly way—and I listened, spellbound. The more I heard, the more inspired and excited I became. He was talking about trees! That the tree is man's best friend. It supplies food to eat, shade on a sunny day, wood to burn in winter, boards to build houses and furniture and boats. The greatest joy is to plant a tree, care for it, and watch it grow. What he did not say was something I had learned in school: that trees purify the air and contribute to the ecology of the planet!

Then, before I knew it, he was gone! But I had changed! I no longer wanted to be an astronaut; I wanted to grow trees!

I ran home with my two remaining pears and my magazines, which no longer interested me.

My father was in his study. "What is it, son? You look as if you've had an epiphany." He was always using words we didn't know, expecting us to look them up in the dictionary. I'm afraid I never did.

With great excitement I told him the whole story. To his credit as a parent, he didn't say I had fallen asleep and dreamed it . . . or I had eaten too many pears . . . or I had read too many weird stories. He said, "Well, son, everything the old fellow said makes sense. If we don't stop destroying trees without replacing them, planet Earth will be in bad trouble. Why don't you and I do something about it? We'll be business partners. You find a forester who'll give us some advice about tree farming. I'll supply the capital to buy seedlings. And you'll be in charge of planting and maintenance."

My father was a wise man. One thing led to another, and I became a partner in his medical clinic, just as he had been my partner in growing trees. But that's not the end of the story. In med school I studied German as the language of science, and that's where I met my future wife. We went to Germany on our honeymoon—to practice our second language. I particularly wanted to visit the Black Forest.

In a shop specializing in wood carvings, I suddenly looked up and saw the little old man who had communicated with me in the woods. He had a long flowing mustache and a Tyrolean hat with the brim pulled down over his eyes, and he was

▼▼▼

carved from a rich mellow wood with some of the tree bark still visible on the hat.

"*Was ist das?*" I asked.

"A wood spirit," the shopkeeper answered in flawless English. "He inhabits trees and brings good luck to those who believe in him. This one was carved by a local artist."

"How did he know what a wood spirit looks like?" Nell asked.

The shopkeeper looked at her pityingly. "Everyone knows."

I wanted to tell him I'd had a close encounter with a wood spirit but held my tongue—to avoid another pitying look. The carving now hangs over my fireplace, reminding me of the day that changed my life. Was I hallucinating? Or had I eaten too many pears? Or what.

7.

My Great-Grandmother's Coal Mine

She Wore a Little White Lace Collar and Carried a Shotgun

How many mining buffs know that one of Moose County's ten coal mines was operated by a woman—more successfully than some men were doing? She said she was only carrying on the work of her late husband. Maggie Sprenkle tells this story regarding her great-grandmother Bridget.

—JMQ

This story about pioneer days in Moose County has been handed down in my family and I believe it to be absolutely true. There were heroes and villains in our history, and many of them were involved in mining.

As you know, there were ten mines in operation—and enough coal for all—but most of the owners were greedy, exploiting their workers shamefully. My great-grandfather, Patrick Borleston, owned the Big B mine. He and another owner, Seth Dimsdale, cared about their workers' health, safety, and families, and their attitude paid off in loyalty and productivity. Their competitors

▼▼▼

were envious to the point of hostility. When Patrick was killed in a carriage accident, his workers were convinced that someone had purposely spooked his horses.

They suspected Ned Bucksmith, owner of the Buckshot mine. Immediately he tried to buy the Big B from the widow. But Bridget was a strong woman. She said she'd operate it herself. The idea of a woman mine operator shocked the other owners, and when the mother of three proceeded to do a man's job better than they could, their antagonism grew—especially that of Ned Bucksmith. She was twice his size, being tall, buxom, and broad-shouldered. She always wore a long, voluminous black dress with a little white lace collar and a pancake hat tied under her chin with ribbons.

Folks said it was the lace collar and ribbons that sent Ned Bucksmith over the edge. He and the other mine owners met in the back room of the K Saloon on Thursday evenings to drink whiskey and play cards, and he got them plotting against Big Bridget. One Thursday night a window was broken in the shack she used for an office. The next week a giant tree was felled across her access road.

▼▼▼

Next her night watchman put out a fire that could have burned down the office.

One Thursday morning Bridget was sitting at her rolltop desk when she heard a frantic banging on the door. There on the doorstep was a young boy, out of breath from running. "Them men!" he gasped. "At the saloon. They be blowin' up your mine!" Then he dashed away.

That evening Bridget went to the saloon in her tentlike black dress and pancake hat, carrying a shotgun. She barged in, knocked over a few chairs, and shouted, "Where are those dirty rats?" Customers hid under tables as she swept toward the back room. "Who's gonna blow up my mine?" she thundered and pointed the gun at Ned Bucksmith. He went out the window headfirst, and the other men piled out the back door. She followed them and unloaded a few warning shots.

There was no more trouble at the Big B. Now if you're wondering about the youngster who tipped her off, he was Ned Bucksmith's boy, and he had a crush on Bridget's daughter. When they grew up, they were married, and that young boy became my grandfather.

▼▼▼

8.

The True (?) History of Squunk Water

—According to Haley Babcock,
Retired Land Surveyor

I met him in the bar at the Black Bear Café. I was waiting for a burger and sipping Squunk water with a lemon twist; he was drinking it neat. He leaned over and said, "Good stuff you're drinkin', mister. I been drinkin' it all my life, and I'm ninety." I protested that he didn't look a day over seventy, and he showed his driver's license for proof. "Yup! I were a tiny tot when my grampa discovered Squunk water. . . ." Mr. Babcock wanted to talk, and I put my tape recorder on the bar.

—JMQ

Well, now, my grampa's farm was all rocky pasture. Not a bush in sight. Gramma tried plantin' vines to shade the front porch, but they grew poorly. Then one day Grampa went to live-stock market and come home with some little green twigs. He'd given a Canadian feller a dollar for 'em. Fast growin' and healthy for livestock, he said.

Well, sir! They growed a foot the first day. In two weeks they covered the dang porch and started over the roof. Grampa cut 'em back, and, by golly, they crawled across the yard to the dog kennel. Afore we knew it, they were all over the outhouse and the fence. All that summer the family had to fight 'em with axes. You couldn't find the front door.

Grampa wished he had his dollar back again—and no vines. He hoped the snow and ice would kill 'em over the winter. The dratted vines just went to sleep and woke up livelier than ever. Filled the drainage ditch! Crept across the road! Got Grampa in trouble with the county road people.

Then one day Grampa heard a bubblin' and gurglin' in the ditch! He put down a pipe and pumped up the cleanest, purest water you ever tasted! The county people tested it and said it was full of healthy minerals. Neighbors started comin' with jugs to fill up—free. Then somebody told Grampa he should bottle it and sell it.

Funny thing, though. The livestock—they wouldn't have nothin' to do with them pesky vines!

JMQ postscript: I later told the bar keeper what I had decided: Mr. Babcock was a shill to promote the sale of Squunk water. As for his look of eternal youth . . . a driver's license can be falsified. Still, I've been consuming more of the stuff lately.

▼▼▼

9.

Whooping It Up
with the Loggers

From a Speech by Roger MacGillivray

Roger, a reporter-photographer for the Moose County Something, formerly taught history in the public schools. "I fed the kids salty bits of lumberjack lore to keep them awake," he says. Lately, Roger has been a consultant to history reenactment groups.
—JMQ

You can't blame the lumberjacks for whooping it up on Saturday night. All week they worked long hours, and it was hard labor. Dangerous, too. The cry of "Timber-r-r!" meant a falling tree. A logger, dashing to get out of the way, might trip over a tree root.

In winter they worked in freezing cold and deep snow as loads of logs were hauled along skid roads on ox-drawn sledges, to wait for the spring thaw. With their boots full of snow and wet socks, they felled trees, loaded the logs, built the skid roads, drove the oxen.

But they were young! Many were in their late

▼▼▼

teens. They did it for adventure—and something to boast about in future years.

They lived on beans and salt pork, turnips, hardtack, and strong tea boiled with molasses. No booze or fist-fighting were allowed in the lumber camps.

At the end of the day they bunked down in a shanty around a potbellied stove—as many as forty men in one room, with forty pairs of wet socks hanging around the stove. Try that on your olfactory senses! And how about snoring? They say it sounded like the Hallelujah Chorus!

But they were young.

On Saturday night they collected their pay and hiked to the nearest lumbertown that had a saloon and a church. Some of the young fellows attended church socials and met nice girls; they were logging to earn enough money to buy a farm. The majority, they say, went to the saloon to blow their week's pay. They bought drinks, played cards, had fistfights, and bantered with the women who hung around.

If one of their buddies drank too much and passed out, they carried him outside and nailed his boots to the wooden sidewalk.

▼▼▼

There was always a derelict at the bar who would do anything for a drink: swallow a live minnow or bite the head off a live chipmunk.

Then there is the story about the drinking pal who died (cause of death is not on record). They took up a collection to buy him a coffin, but he couldn't be buried until spring; the ground was frozen. Meanwhile he was in the deep-freeze shed behind the furniture store, which was also the undertaking establishment. The friends of the deceased thought it would be only right and proper to bring him back for one last time—to the place where he had spent so many happy hours. A task force was sent to break into the undertaker's shed. The coffin was propped against the bar. Everyone rose and drank a solemn toast to good old Joe.

This actually happened. What can you say? It was more than a hundred years ago. And they were young.

▼▼▼

10.

"The Princess" and the Pirates

A Legend from the Days of Sailing Ships

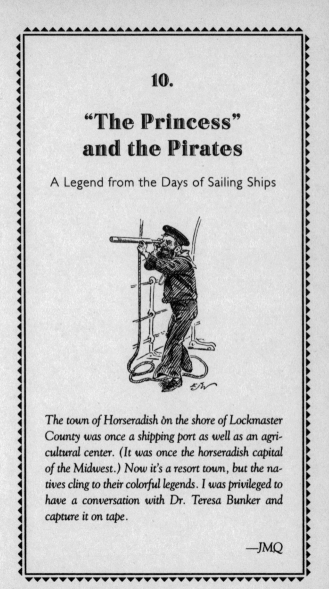

The town of Horseradish on the shore of Lockmaster County was once a shipping port as well as an agricultural center. (It was once the horseradish capital of the Midwest.) Now it's a resort town, but the natives cling to their colorful legends. I was privileged to have a conversation with Dr. Teresa Bunker and capture it on tape.

—JMQ

I s it true, Dr. Bunker, that horseradish fumes still
linger and make an invigorating atmosphere for
tourists?"

"Absolutely, but please call me Tess."

"Were your forebears horseradish farmers?"

"No, they were in shipping. Our town was the
chief port for all of Lockmaster County, and my
great-grandfather's adventures as captain of the
sailing vessel *Princess* have made him a legendary
figure. You see, all sorts of commodities were being shipped in and out. There was still some gold-
mining in the interior, as well as a thriving fur
trade, especially beaver. This made cargo ships

▼▼▼

prey to buccaneers. Did you know there were pirates on the lakes at one time?"

"Your cousin told me that their victims were often made to walk the plank. He never mentioned the *Princess*."

"Oh, she was famous in her day! On one occasion the *Princess* sailed out of harbor with a cargo and had just lost sight of land when a craft with a black flag loomed on the horizon. Captain Bunker gave some unusual orders: When the pirate ship hove to, the crew would go below with crowbars and wet rags.

"A volley was fired across the bow of the *Princess*, and she dropped sail. Then all hands disappeared into the hold, which was stowed with kegs of grated horseradish mixed with vinegar. The pirates came aboard, stomping and cursing. Where was the blankety-blank crew? It was a blankety-blank ghost ship! They stormed down the hatch. . . . Immediately the lids came off the kegs, and the fumes rose like poison gas! The pirates choked and staggered blindly, while the crew—masked with wet rags—threw handfuls of the stuff and swung their crowbars. Overpowered,

▼▼▼

the pirates were dragged to the deck and heaved overboard.

"The pirate story is true, but there are many Bunyanesque tales about our town, like the cargo ship powered by horseradish fumes before steam boilers came into use."

▼▼▼

11.

Wildcattin' with
an Old Hog

The Recollections of an "Old Hoghead"

I first met Ozzie Penn in a retirement center for rail-roadmen—and immediately turned on my tape recorder. He spoke the Old Moose dialect, which still falls pleasantly on the ear. He had the engineer's symbolic gold watch—a reward for always coming in on time.

—JMQ

Y ou were a master of your craft, I'm told. What does it take to make a good engineer?"

"L'arnin' to start up slow and stop smooth. . . . L'arnin' to keep yer head when it be hell on the rails. . . . Prayin' to God fer a good fireman. . . . And abidin' by rule G."

"What's the fireman's job on a steam locomotive?"

"He be the one stokes the firebox an' keeps the boiler steamin'. Takes a good crew to make a good run and come in on time. Spent my whole life comin' in on time. Eleventh commandment, it were called. Now, here I be, an' time don't mean nothin'."

▼▼▼

"Why was it so important to be on time?"

"Made money for the comp'ny. Made wrecks, too . . . takin' chances, takin' shortcuts."

"Were you in many wrecks?"

"Yep, an' on'y jumped once. I were a youngun, deadheadin' to meet a crew in Flapjack. High-ballin' round a curve, we run into a rockslide. Engineer yelled 'Jump!' an' I jumped. Fireman jumped, too. Engineer were killed."

"What do you know about the famous wreck at Wildcat, Ozzie?"

"That were afore my time, but I heerd plenty o' tales in the SC and L switchyard. In them days the yard had eighteen tracks and a roundhouse for twenty hogs.

"The town weren't called Wildcat in them days. It were South Fork. Trains from up north slowed down to twenty at South Fork afore goin' down a steep grade to a mighty bad curve and a wood trestle bridge. The rails, they be a hun'erd feet over the water. One day a train come roarin' through South Fork, full steam, whistle screechin'. It were a wildcat—a runaway train—headed for the gorge. At the bottom—crash!—bang! Then hissin' steam.

▼▼▼

Then dead quiet. Then the screamin' started. Fergit how many killed, but it were the worst ever!"

"Did they ever find out what caused the wreck?"

"Musta been the brakes went blooey, but the railroad, they laid it on the engineer—said he were drinkin'. Saved the comp'ny money, it did, to lay it on the engineer. Poor feller! Steam boiler exploded, an' he were scalded to death."

"Horrible!"

"Yep. It were bad, 'cause he weren't a drinkin' man."

"So that's why they changed the name of the town to Wildcat! You're a very lucky man, Ozzie, to have survived so many dangers! If you had your life to live over again, would you be a hoghead?"

"Yep."

▼▼▼

12.

The Scratching
Under the Door

As Recalled by Emma Huggins Wimsey,
Age Eighty-nine

She was a frail little woman in a wheelchair when I interviewed her at a family reunion. A caregiver had brought her from the Senior Care Facility in order to maintain her record: She had not missed a reunion since the age of two. Emma's eyes still sparkled with loving memories when she talked about her cat, Punkin.

—JMQ

When I was a little girl I had a cat named Punkin because she was orange. Such a dear kitty! We had a game we played. After my mother put me to bed each night and closed the bedroom door, Punkin would come and scratch under the door as if she was trying to get in. I'd jump out of bed and grab her paw. She'd pull it away and stick another paw under the door. Oh, we had such fun! And we never got caught. We played our secret game all the time I was growing up.

Punkin and I were secret conspirators for many years. Then she passed away, and I went away to

▼▼▼

teacher's college—or normal school, as it used to be called. Schoolteaching in those days was the only respectable work for a respectable young woman to do. Students lived in dormitories, and that's where I first experienced a strange incident.

In the middle of the night I woke up and heard a familiar scratching under the door. How could it be? Punkin was dead—and buried under the old oak tree. And then I smelled smoke! I dragged my roommate out of the bed and screamed, "The building's on fire!" We ran down the hall in our nightclothes, banging on doors and shouting "Fire! Fire!"

The firewagon came and poured on buckets of water, and the dormitory was saved. And I was honored in assembly for detecting the danger and rousing my fellow students. Imagine that! I didn't tell them about Punkin. They would have laughed at me.

I never told anyone about Punkin—not even my husband. We lived in a comfortable farm-house, where we were raising a family. Then one windy night I woke up again and heard scratching under the door. I woke up my husband, and he

▼▼▼

jumped out of bed and shouted, "Take the children down in the basement!" It was a tornado, and it took the roof off our house, but the family was safe. Of course, I never said a word about Punkin.

There was another time, too, when a burglar got in the house in the middle of the night . . . but I'm getting tired . . .

Postscript: A short note came from a caregiver at the Senior Care Facility. "It is our sad duty to inform you that Emma Huggins Wimsey passed away last night at 4:30 A.M. She had just turned ninety and was alert and cheerful all day. Shortly before the end dear Emma said, "I hear Punkin scratching under the door."

13.

The Dimsdale Jinx

Homer Tibbitt Tells about the Village That Disappeared

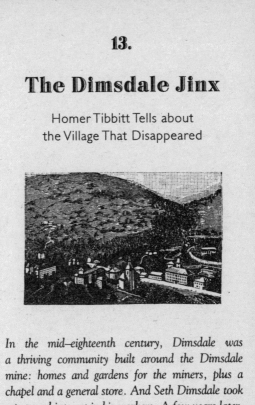

In the mid–eighteenth century, Dimsdale was a thriving community built around the Dimsdale mine: homes and gardens for the miners, plus a chapel and a general store. And Seth Dimsdale took a paternal interest in his workers. A few years later, it was all gone. What happened? Our county historian knows the answer.

—JMQ

It started about a hundred years ago, when the mines were going full blast, and this was the richest county in the state. This isn't a tall tale, mind you. It's true. It isn't short either.

There was a miner named Roebuck Magley, a husky man in his late forties who worked in the Dimsdale mine. He had a wife and three sons, and they lived in one of the cottages provided for workers. Not all mine owners exploited their workers, you know. Seth Dimsdale was successful but not greedy. He saw to it that every family had a decent place to live and a plot for a vegetable garden, and he gave them the seed to plant. There was also a company doctor who looked after the families without charge.

Roebuck worked hard, and the boys went to work in the mines as soon as they finished eighth grade. Betty Magley worked hard, too, feeding her men, scrubbing their clothes, pumping water, tending the garden, and making their shirts. But somehow she always stayed pretty.

Suddenly Roebuck fell sick and died. He'd been complaining about stomach pains, and one day he came home from work, ate his supper, and dropped dead. Things like that happened in those days, and folks accepted them. Men were asphyxiated in the mines, blown to bits in explosions, or they came home and dropped dead. Nobody sued for negligence.

Roebuck's death certificate, signed by Dr. Penfield, said "Heart failure". Seth Dimsdale paid Mrs. Magley a generous sum from the insurance policy he carried on his workers, and she was grateful. She'd been ailing herself, and the company doctor was at a loss to diagnose her symptoms.

Well, about a month later her eldest son, Robert, died in the mine shaft of "respiratory failure", ac-

▼▼▼

cording to the death certificate, and it wasn't long before the second son, Amos, died under the same circumstances. The miners' wives flocked around Betty Magley and tried to comfort her, but there was unrest among the men. They grumbled about "bad air". One Sunday they marched to the mine office, shouting and brandishing pickaxes and shovels. Seth Dimsdale was doing all he could to maintain safe working conditions, considering the technology of the times, so he authorized a private investigation.

Both Robert and Amos had died, he learned, after eating their lunch pasties underground; Roebuck's last meal had been a large pasty in his kitchen. The community was alarmed. "Bad meat!" they said. Those tasty meat-and-potato stews wrapped in a thick lard crust were the staple diet of miners and their families.

Then something curious happened to Alfred, the youngest son. While underground, he shared his pasty with another miner whose lunch had fallen out of his pocket when he was climbing down the ladder. Soon both men were complaining of pains, nausea, and numb hands and feet.

▼▼▼

The emergency whistle blew, and the two men were hauled up the ladder in the "basket", as the rescue contraption was called.

When word reached Seth Dimsdale, he notified the prosecuting attorney in Pickax, and the court issued an order to exhume the bodies of Roebuck, Robert, and Amos. Their internal organs, sent to the toxicologist at the state capital, were found to contain lethal quantities of arsenic, and Mrs. Magley was questioned by the police.

At that point, neighbors started whispering: "Could she have poisoned her own family? Where did she get the poison?" Arsenic could be used to kill insects in vegetable gardens, but people were afraid to use it. Then the neighbors remembered the doctor's visits to treat Mrs. Magley's mysterious ailment. He visited almost every day.

When Dr. Penfield was arrested, the mining community was bowled over. He was a handsome man with a splendid mustache, and he cut a fine figure in his custom-made suits and derby hats. He lived in a big house and owned one of the first automobiles. His wife was considered a snob, but

▼▼▼

Dr. Penfield had a good bedside manner and was much admired.

It turned out, however, that he was in debt for his house and car, and his visits to treat the pretty Betty Magley were more personal than professional. He was the first defendant placed on trial. Mrs. Magley sat in jail and awaited her turn.

The miners, convinced of the integrity of the doctor, rose to his support, and it was difficult to seat an unbiased jury. The trial itself lasted longer than any in local history, and when it was over, the county was broke. Twice its annual budget had been spent on the court proceedings.

The story revealed at the trial was one of greed and passion. Dr. Penfield had supplied the arsenic—for medical purposes, he said, and any overdose was caused by human error. Mrs. Magley had baked the pasties and collected the insurance money, giving half to the doctor. He was found guilty on three counts of murder and sentenced to life in prison.

Mrs. Magley was never tried for the crime because the county couldn't afford a second trial.

▼▼▼

The commissioners said it wasn't "worth the candle", as the saying went. It would be better if she just left town, quietly.

So she disappeared, along with her youngest son, the only one to survive. Seth Dimsdale retired to Ohio and also disappeared. The Dimsdale mine disappeared. The whole town of Dimsdale disappeared. It was called the Dimsdale Jinx.

14.

The Mystery of Dank Hollow

A True Story of Pioneer Days,
Circa 1850

The tale is corroborated by the discovery of a diary belonging to the pastor who heard the dying man's last words. The diary is now in the historical collection of the public library. I am indebted to Silas Dingwall for permission to tape his account.

—JMQ

One day a young fisherman by the name of Wallace Reekie, who lived in the village here, went to his brother's funeral in a town twenty miles away. He didn't have a horse, so he set out on foot at daybreak and told his new bride he'd be home at nightfall. Folks didn't like to travel that road after dark because there was a dangerous dip in it. Mists rose up and hid the path, you see, and it was easy to make a wrong turn and walk into the bog. They called it Dank Hollow.

At the funeral, Wallace helped carry his brother's casket to the burial place in the woods, and on the way he tripped over a tree root. There

▼▼▼

was an old Scottish superstition: Stumble while carrying a corpse, and you'll be the next to go into the grave. It must have troubled Wallace, because he drank too much at the wake and was late in leaving for home. His relatives wanted him to stay over, but he was afraid his young wife would worry. He took a nap before leaving, though, and got a late start.

It was a five-hour trek, and when he didn't show up by nightfall, like he'd said, his wife sat up all night, praying. It was just turning daylight when she was horrified to see her husband staggering into the dooryard of their little hut. Before he could say a word, he collapsed on the ground. She screamed for help, and a neighbor's boy ran for the doctor. He came galloping on horseback and did what he could. They also called the pastor of the church. He put his ear to the dying man's lips and listened to his last babbling words, but for some reason he never told what he heard.

From then on, folks dreaded the Dank Hollow after dark. It was not only because of the mists and the bog but because of Wallace's mysterious death. That happened way back, of course. By 1930,

▼▼▼

when a paved road bypassed the Hollow, the incident was mostly forgotten. And then, in 1970, the pastor's descendants gave his diary to the Trawnto Historical Society. That's when the whole story came to light.

Wallace had reached the Dank Hollow after dark and was feeling his way cautiously along the path, when he was terrified to see a line of shadowy beings coming toward him out of the bog. One of them was his brother, who had just been buried. They beckoned Wallace to join their ghostly procession, and that was the last thing the poor man remembered. How he had found his way home in his delirium was hard to explain.

The pastor had written in his diary: "Only the prayers of his wife and his great love for her could have guided him." And then he added a strange thing: "When Wallace collapsed in his dooryard, all his clothes were inside out."

15.

Tale of
Two Tombstones

As the Stonecutter Told It
to His Grandson

Thornton Haggis said, "Gramps wouldn't want this printed because it involves a customer, and he was punctilious about such things. But all of them are long gone, so . . . what the heck! Just change the names." The following was taped for this volume.

—JMQ

This was before I was born, but my dad told me after I started getting interested in local history. After World War One, he said, the stonecutting business wasn't doing too well. The mines had closed; the county had been lumbered over, and there was an economic bust and general exodus. Thousands were going Down Below to work in factories—and to die there, apparently. At any rate, they weren't coming north to be buried. He had a Model T truck and did some hauling jobs to make ends meet, but it was rough. People were living on oatmeal and turnips, and families were having to double up.

▼▼▼

Then, one day Ben Dibble came in to order a tombstone for his uncle, who'd been living with them. The old fellow had been struck down by lightning and was being buried on the farm. Dad chiseled a stone and delivered it in his truck—all Ben had was an oxcart—and the two of them set up the stone on a fresh grave by the river. Dad was glad to get the business; his family was in need of shoes, and Ben paid cash.

In a week or so, Ben was back for another stone; his aunt had died of a broken heart. Dad cut the stone and, while delivering it, wondered about burying somebody on a riverbank. What if there was a flood? . . . Anyway, he and Ben set up the stone, and Ben asked to look at the truck; he was thinking of buying one. To Dad's embarrassment, it wouldn't start! He tinkered with the motor until the farm bell called Ben in to supper.

As soon as Ben had left, Dad sneaked back to the graves. He'd only pretended the truck wouldn't start. Scraping the topsoil away, he found some loose planks, and under the planks he found cases of booze! Old Log Cabin whiskey from Canada.

▼▼▼

Rumrunners were bringing it across the lake and up the river, where it was stashed on Ben's farm until it could be delivered Down Below. Well! Dad had three options: report 'em, ignore 'em, or join 'em. Prohibition was bringing prosperity back to Moose County. People were flocking north by the trainload, and everybody was smuggling contraband in from Canada or out by train and Model T. Some of today's old families who claim to be descended from lumber barons or mining tycoons are really descended from bootleggers.

I can honestly say I'm the son of a stonecutter. Dad was too busy cutting stone to break the law. He said the tombstone business was very good during Prohibition. All I know is that all of us kids had shoes and went away to college.

▼▼▼

16.

The Pork-and-Beans Incident at Boggy Bottom

As Confirmed by the County Historian

Homer Tibbitt, who taught in a one-room school-house in the 1930s, knew the hero of this tale and also the junior-grade terrorist.

—JMQ

Wesley Prescott was a good kid. Studied hard but would rather be playing baseball. Finished the eighth grade but dropped out because the high school was thirteen miles away, and there was no public transportation. Also, Moose County had been in a depression ever since the mines closed before World War One. People had left in droves, to seek work in cities Down Below. So . . .

Mr. Prescott, a skilled carpenter and house-builder, had gone to Detroit to look for any kind of work, leaving his wife and three kids in the

▼▼▼

small village of Isbey. He wrote to them weekly—
no luck. They were living mainly on oatmeal and
turnips. The church had a cow, and Wesley
would go there with a jug—and stay to muck the
barn.

Then the first money came from Detroit, and
Mr. Prescott wrote: "I got a job as a White Wing.
You should see me in my white suit." They never
dreamed that he was a street sweeper. Mrs.
Prescott made out a shopping list for Wesley to
take to the general store in Fishport. It was a
three-mile walk in each direction, but he was
used to that. Now, at age fifteen, he was the man
of the household and took his responsibilities se-
riously. It was Saturday afternoon, and he even
offered to give up his weekly ball game with a
scrub team in a vacant lot behind the church, but
his mother said he could do the shopping after
the game, if he didn't dawdle. She knew how
much baseball meant to him. It was hardball, and
he was a champ at hitting, running, fielding, and
catching men off bases with a swift, straight

▼▼▼

throw. People predicted that Wesley would land in the big leagues but suggested that he change his name to something more shoutable in the bleachers.

So Wesley had his nine innings before hiking to the Fishport General Store with his list: more oatmeal, more turnips, but also potatoes, onions, flour, molasses, barley, and—for a treat— four cans of salt pork and beans with tomato sauce.

The groceries filled the largest brown paper bag in the store—about a bushel of them. And heavy! Wesley decided to take the shortcut home, although his mother wouldn't approve. It was only a mile and a half but through back country. A trail ran through a wooded area and down into a gully called Boggy Bottom; there was swampland on either side of the footpath. Shadowed by ancient trees and tangled vines, it was gloomy at any time of day but scary at twilight.

It was twilight when Wesley reached Boggy

Bottom. All was still. And then he heard a moaning sound. Hugging the bagful of food with both arms, he plodded on. Then he heard a human cry, and an apparition rose from a clump of bushes—white except for two hollow eyes. It came closer, making unearthly sounds.

With great deliberation Wesley set the loaded bag down in the path, braced between his legs, and hurled a can of pork and beans swiftly and accurately at the pair of haunting eyes.

The apparition crashed into the bushes with a howl of pain, and Wesley picked up his load and trudged home.

As Mrs. Prescott unloaded the groceries, she said, "I thought I ordered four cans."

"That's all they had," Wesley said. It was the first time he had ever fibbed to his mother.

Meanwhile, a youth with a broken nose staggered into Fishport. This was the end of the scary happenings at Boggy Bottom. This small-town terrorist had been spooking nervous trav-

▼▼▼

elers and causing them to drop everything and run.

As for the Prescott family, they eventually got back on their feet, and—yes—Wesley got into the major leagues, but he changed his name.

17.

At Last, a Hospital in the Wilderness

Ten Beds, Two Nurses, Many Volunteers!

The early medical history of Moose County could not have been written without the support of the women's auxiliary—those dedicated volunteers—sewing, visiting patients, supplying them with books and magazines, bringing fruit and flowers, and, of course, fund-raising.

—JMQ

Those were days when women wore high lace collars and skirts that swept the sidewalk, not to mention hats of prodigious size. Horse-and-buggy traffic thronged the main street of "bright, busy, bustling Pickax", as the picture postcards labeled it. This was the local scene when the auxiliary was formed.

The minutes of the first meeting still exist in a yellowed ledger, written in old-fashioned script with a nib pen. "At a meeting of the Ladies of the City of Pickax, held on June 25, A.D. 1906, the following ladies were present." There follows a list of forty names, a veritable Who's Who of Pickax.

▼▼▼

Dues were fixed at a dollar a year, payable quarterly, and officers were elected.

A Work Committee was immediately organized to make gowns for the patients, and also for the nurses to wear in the operating room.

A Soliciting Committee got busy, and contributions started to come in from other organizations, whereupon the Purchasing Committee bought such amenities as cushions, hassocks, and a baby basket. The Work Committee covered the cushions and made leggings for the patients to wear on the operating table. They also covered two bricks, according to the minutes of August 6, 1906, the purpose of which was not disclosed.

The Literature Committee arranged for subscriptions to *Collier's* and *Leslie's* magazines, and a member donated a copy of a book that had been a best-seller since 1901: *Mrs. Wiggs of the Cabbage Patch.*

The Purchasing Committee then bought an invalid's chair for $18—and a blanket for it, costing $2.25. The Work Committee kept on sewing: sheets, pillowcases, doilies for the sideboard, napkins, bedspreads, more towels, more bandages.

▼▼▼

Meanwhile, the Ways and Means Committee bubbled with ideas. They considered selling postcard views of the hospital. They thought about publishing a cookbook, or a "receipt book", as it was called in those days. They staged a social affair called a "10-cent coffee" and cleared $12.70 for the treasury. An ice-cream social brought in $12. A Tag Day and a public supper helped support the hospital's needs.

A crying need was a mangle for the laundry room, but it would cost $116—an enormous sum, it seemed. All efforts were then concentrated on the Mangle Fund. A Junior Auxiliary of eighty-six young people was formed to help raise money. On March 13, thirteen hostesses invited guests to thirteen "13-cent coffees" and realized $15.06. The first charity ball in 1908 netted the princely sum of $72.89.

Meanwhile, committees had been organized in other towns. Their particular responsibility was the hospital pantry, and they worked hard at canning home-grown fruits and vegetables and making jellies for the pantry shelves.

Not only was the Auxiliary able to purchase

▼▼▼

that mangle, but they raised money for the first electric appliances: first, an electric iron for the laundry room, then in 1911 the first electric washing machine.

And the Work Committee kept on sewing!

18.

Emmaline and the Spiral Staircase

Both Have Been Gone for a Hundred Years, But...

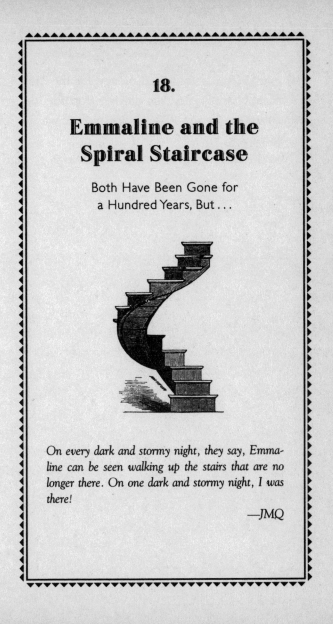

On every dark and stormy night, they say, Emmaline can be seen walking up the stairs that are no longer there. On one dark and stormy night, I was there!

—JMQ

On the farm and adjoining the Goodwinter Farmhouse museum there is an old Victorian mansion with a tower built by Captain Fugtree, an American war hero of the nineteenth century. He had a daughter, Emmaline, who was in love with Samson Goodwinter. Her father, not thinking highly of the Goodwinters, forbade her to see Samson. Nevertheless, Emmaline would go into the tower and signal the Goodwinter farmhouse, and the lovers would meet on the banks of the creek.

Then Samson was thrown from his horse and killed, and two weeks later, their child was born. Considering the mind-set of that period in history

▼▼▼

it's possible to imagine that the baby was taken away, and the young mother was shunned by family and friends. One thing is known: Emmaline went to the tower "on a dark and stormy night", opened a window, and jumped to her death. Her infuriated father responded by ripping out the spiral staircase and replacing it with a conventional flight of stairs.

Now flash-forward a hundred years or more. Emmaline's granddaughter, Kristi, is living in the old house and raising goats. And on every dark and stormy night she turns off the lights and watches the shadowy form of her grandmother ascending the spiral stairs—the stairs that were ripped out long ago. "She's so beautiful," Kristi murmurs. On one occasion the new museum manager and myself were honored by an invitation to the solemn event, and we agreed with Kristi that Emmaline was beautiful.

We said good night and left Kristi in a state of radiant transfixation.

On the way back to the museum, we walked in silence for a while until I said, "It was an interesting evening."

▼▼▼

"Yeah," he said, "but the house was kind of damp and chilly." There was another silence before he blurted, "Tell me honestly, Qwill. Did you see Emmaline?"

I took a deep breath and said, "No. . . . Did you?"

"Not really."

▼▼▼

19.

The Curious Fate of the *Jenny Lee*

Commercial Fishermen Think They Know What Happened

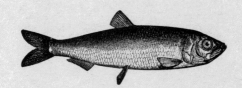

John Bushland, a commercial photographer, was showing off his new cabin cruiser, the View Finder, *and we anchored in a cove for a picnic lunch. I said, "For a landlubber, Bushy, you know your way around the lake pretty well." He not only corrected me, but an enlightening conversation ensued. As usual, I had a tape recorder in my pocket, and I let him do most of the talking.*

—JMQ

You've got me wrong, Qwill. I was born and brought up near the lake. I relocated in Lockmaster when I married. Believe me, it's good to be back here. I have a passion for fishing and boating. You probably never heard this, but my family was in commercial fishing for three generations before my grandfather sold out to the Scottens. He was always telling me about the herring business in the twenties and thirties. They used wooden boats and cotton nets—and no echo sounders or radio phones. You wouldn't believe what fishermen went through in those days."

▼▼▼

"Try me," I said, always curious about someone else's business.

"Well, the Bushland Fisheries regularly shipped hundred-pound kegs of dried salted herring Down Below, salt being the preservative in those days, before refrigeration. And here's the interesting part: The kegs went to Pennsylvania, West Virginia, and other coal-producing states, and the miners practically lived on herring. They could buy it for four cents a pound. The fishermen got a penny a pound and worked their tails off to get it. They were up before dawn, out on the lake in open boats in all kinds of weather, hauling heavy nets till their backs nearly broke, filling the boats to the gunnels with fish, and racing back to shore to dress it. Sometimes they worked half the night— salting it, packing it, and loading it on a freight car before the locomotive backed up and hauled the car away."

I said, "I hope they didn't use gill nets."

"No way! They used coarse-mesh 'pond' nets. That's spelled p-o-u-n-d. I never found out why it was pronounced the way it was. In the spring, after the ice broke up, they drove stakes in the lake bottom—tree trunks as long as fifty feet—and they drove 'em with manpower before the gasoline derrick came into use. After that, they set out their nets and visited them every day to scoop out the catch. When cold weather came, they pulled up the stakes before the ice could crush 'em. Then they spent the winter mending nets and repairing boats."

"I can see why your grandfather wanted to get out of the business."

"That wasn't the reason. He wasn't afraid of hard work. It's a sad story. He lost his father and two older brothers in a freak incident on the lake. They went out in a thirty-five-foot boat, the *Jenny Lee*, to lift nets. The weather was fair. Lots of boats were in the fishing grounds, all within sight of each other. Suddenly the *Jenny Lee* vanished. One minute she was seen by other fishermen; the next minute she was gone. The authorities searched for a week and never found the bodies—never even found the boat underwater. The whole village of Fishport was in mourning. It's remained an unsolved mystery."

I stared at Bushy sternly. "Is this an actual fact?"

"It's the God's truth! There's a memorial plaque

in the churchyard. Someone wrote a folk song about it."

"Were there any speculations as to what happened?"

"All kinds, but there was only one conclusion, and you won't like it. It had to have something to do with the Visitors—like, they could make a thirty-five-foot boat vaporize. There was lots of talk about the Visitors way back then, you know: Blobs of green light in the night sky . . . Sometimes shining things in daylight. That was before I was born, and they're still coming back—some years more than others."

I wanted to believe my friend, but found it difficult. I said, "You once told me about some kind of incident when you were out fishing."

"Yeah, it was my old boat. I was on the lake all by myself, fishing for bass. All at once I had a strange feeling I wasn't alone. I looked up, and there was a silver disk with portholes! I had my camera case with me, but before I could get out my camera, the thing disappeared in a flash. Their speed, you know, has been clocked at seventeen hundred miles per hour."

▼▼▼

I listened with my usual skepticism, although I tried not to show it. I thought, Here I am in the middle of the lake with a crazy guy! Watch it!

Soberly, I asked, "Do they accelerate from zero to seventeen hundred in the blink of an eye? Or do you think they have a technology that makes them invisible at will?"

"That's the mystery," Bushy said.

"And there's another mystery. There's a rash of sightings every seven years—documented in diaries and county records as far back as 1850. Does it take them seven years for a round-trip between their planet and our planet? Or is there a time differential? Is our year equivalent to their month?"

I said, "Bushy, we'd better get back to shore. I have to feed the cats."

▼▼▼

20.

A Scary Experience on a Covered Bridge

It Was Dark and Emma Wimsey Was Alone

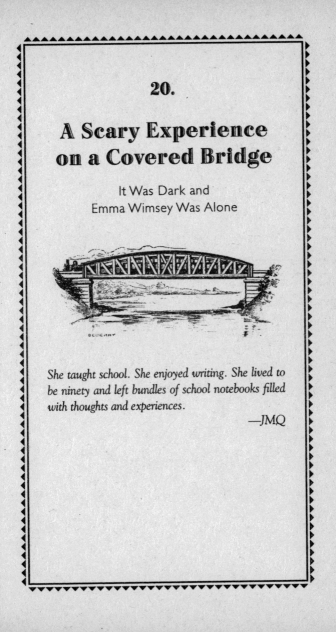

She taught school. She enjoyed writing. She lived to be ninety and left bundles of school notebooks filled with thoughts and experiences.

—JMQ

When I started teaching in a one-room schoolhouse near Black Creek, I lived with a farm family and had to walk three miles to school in all kinds of weather. I always went early because I had to make a fire in the woodstove and trim the lamps and wash the glass chimneys and sweep the floor.

One day in late November before snow had started to turn the brown landscape white, I set out for school in pitch-darkness. There was a covered bridge over the creek, and oh! how I dreaded crossing that bridge in the dark! On this particular day, as I entered the dark tunnel, I saw something

▼▼▼

that made my knees shake. There was a white object at the far end—small and round and white and floating in the air. I stood stock-still with my mouth open as it came closer, bobbing gently. I wanted to turn around and run, but my feet were rooted to the ground. And then I realized it was a *face*—no body, just a white face! It started to make noises: "U-u-ugh! U-u-ugh!"

I tried to scream, but no sound came from my mouth. Then two white hands reached for me. "U-u-ugh! U-u-ugh!"

As the white face came close to mine, I was about to faint, but then I recognized it. I recognized a pale young girl from our church. She was wearing black garments and a black shawl over her head, and she was trying to tell me not to be afraid. She was a deaf-mute.

21.

A Cat Tale: Holy Terror and the Bishop

Told by a Retired Clergyman, the Reverend Arledge Harding

Mr. and Mrs. Harding were vacationing at a bed-and-breakfast on an offshore island, and they were sitting in a porch swing when he told this tale. He was tall and dignified and always wore a French beret, indoors and out. There was a twinkle in his one good eye when he recalled the memorable incident.

—JMQ

I can hardly say that we *had* a Siamese cat, but there was one who accepted bed and board from us—a strong-willed but fascinating creature whom we named Holy Terror. At the time I was vicar of a church in a small town in Indiana, and the parishioners were flattered to hear that the Bishop would be gracing us with his presence in the very near future. Plans were being made to welcome him, and it seemed that an appropriate event would be a private luncheon at the vicarage. Mrs. Harding can serve a charming luncheon, but she always inquires if the guest of honor has likes or dislikes—and how he or she feels about cats.

▼▼▼

The Bishop's office assured us that he was very fond of cats—and also a Bloody Mary before lunch. Unaccustomed as I was to serving drinks, I consulted all available experts and decided on the perfect recipe, after which I took pains to assemble the correct ingredients.

On the appointed day the distinguished guest arrived and was duly greeted, after which I repaired to the kitchen to mix the concoction myself. As I carried the tray into the living room, Holy Terror went into one of his Siamese tizzies, flying up and down stairs and around the house at great speed, until he swooped over my shoulder and landed in the tray. Glasses catapulted into space and the Bloody Mary sprayed tomato juice over the walls, carpet, ceiling, and the august person of the Bishop.

It so happened that our guest was blessed with a congenial sense of humor, and he has been telling the story all over creation for the last thirty years.

▾▾▾

22

Those Pushy Moose County Blueberries

They Seem to Be Saying, "We Were Here First"

Food editor Mildred Riker of the Moose County Something is on their side. This champion of the blueberry even has a "blueberry rake" on her desk, serving as a letter-file. Here's what she had to say for Short & Tall Tales.

—JMQ

Long before we knew about antioxidants and bioflavonoids, blueberries were doing their thing; Mother Nature had made them good-for-you as well as good-to-eat. In the seventeenth century French explorers reported that native Americans used wild blueberries as food and medicine.

In the nineteenth century my great-grandfather, Elias King, came to Moose County from Maine to work as a lumberjack and save up to buy a farm. His diary is preserved in the historical collection at the public library.

He wrote that the woods were full of wild blueberries, called bilberries. The lumberjacks ate them by the handful. They were like candy—after the lumbercamp diet of beans and salt pork.

Eventually he had saved enough to buy farmland at the north edge of what is now Pickax. The land was well endowed with wild blueberries—low-growing shrubs that crept across the property as if they owned it.

When my grandfather, Matthew King, inherited the farm, he claimed that blueberries occupied more acreage than did corn and potatoes. He said, "Wild blueberries can't be cultivated, but they can't be killed, either." So he gave the berries away to anyone who cared to pick them. Grandma King said she laid awake nights thinking of ways to use them in family meals: a handful of blueberries here, a handful of blueberries there. The perfect blueberry pie recipe that she masterminded is in my security box at the bank.

By the time my father inherited the property, the family was involved in producing, packaging, marketing, and shipping blueberry products. He was jocularly called the Blueberry King, and friends launched a frivolous campaign to change the name of the area to Blueberry County. Their slogan: "When was the last time you saw a Moose?"

Finally my brothers and I were bequeathed the blueberry empire, but we were interested in careers of our own. We sold out to the large Toodle family, who developed the property in various ways, including a supermarket with extensive parking and loading facilities. They carry excellent produce from all parts of the country. Included are the large cultivated berries that I put in muffins, pancakes, soups, salads, stews, and Grandma King's blueberry pie. Considering my blueberry heritage, it seems ironic that I now buy the berries in eight-ounce boxes. No matter. There is a postscript to the tale.

The supermarket has had constant trouble with the parking lot. Asphalt buckled. Concrete cracked. One day Grandma Toodle showed me the latest damage. Shrubs were pushing up in the wide cracks.

"What do you think they are?" she asked.

"I know what they are!" I said. "Nothing can stop those pushy Moose County blueberries."

▾▾▾

23.

The Curse on the Apple Orchard

Based on a Taped Conversation with Homer Tibbitt

Homer, retired educator, is now official historian for Moose County. Good choice! He soaks up local history like a sponge to be squeezed upon demand. He has written numerous papers on local history, all on file at the Pickax Public Library.

—JMQ

Foreword: The Trevelyan apple barn will still be standing after the Rock of Gibraltar has crumbled away. Now converted to a residence, it still exudes the aroma of Winesaps and McIntoshes in certain weather. Why it was abandoned remains a mystery. The orchard has withered; the farmhouse has burned down. All that remains is the barn and a lilac bush as big as a two-story, three-bedroom house. In this recording Homer Tibbitt tells all he knows, with only an occasional prodding by the interviewer.

"Trevelyan is a Cornish name. Many folks think it's Welsh. Wrong! The Trevelyans came from Cornwall, England, in the mid–nineteenth century, bringing with them the famous meat-and-potato pasty, which has become the official food of Moose County. The miners used to take them down the mine shaft for lunch; now tourists take them to the beach for picnics. Where do you want me to start?"

"With the orchard—in its heyday."

"It was a typical strip farm, half a mile long, but narrow. It fronted on the back road, now called Trevelyan Road. There was a farmhouse there. The barn was at the other end. In between: nothing but apple trees. The barn was a drive-through, with doors big enough to admit a horse-drawn wagon piled high with apples. Pickax folks considered the barn pretentious. Too big, too showy. Don't know how they felt about the family themselves. Perhaps the Trevelyans mixed only with other Trevelyans—all of whom, I might say, seemed to be hard working and successful.

"Anyhow, the farmhouse was struck by lightning. The farmwife and her youngest child died in

▼▼▼

the fire that destroyed their home. Where was the farmer? Where were the older children? No one knows. They didn't have a real newspaper in those days. That same year all the apple trees began to wither, struck by blight. Then the horses died. People thought they were poisoned. Then the farmer hanged himself from a rafter in the barn. It was a curse, the locals said. No one would touch the property with a ten-foot pole—until Fanny Klingenschoen bought it and let it rot."

"Was there never an investigation?"

"Could be they didn't know what the word meant in those days. The good folk of Pickax concluded it was a curse! That was a handy way of dismissing the whole incident. But you can't help wondering. Did someone have a grudge against the family? Were they too prosperous? Was someone jealous? Had the farmer done some awful thing that had to be avenged?"

▼▼▼

24.

Matilda,
a Family Heroine

Why Was There No Surname
on Her Gravestone?

Lisa Compton, whose maiden name was Campbell, was one of the volunteers who tidied the historic Campbell burial ground this spring, and she called me with an answer to a question that has puzzled her family in the past. This is the whole story, as related by Lisa.

—JMQ

Do you know the Campbell graveyard south of Purple Point, Qwill? It goes back to 1850 and was long ago outgrown. The family keeps it up as a place of solace in troubled times. There was one stone that puzzled me: "Matilda, age 14". Was she not a Campbell? If not, why was she there? Usually the stones are chiseled with all kinds of information: cause of death, names of heirs, even the names of family pets! There was only the date—1897, I think. Was there a scandal?

I'm like you, Qwill. I can't stand to be in the dark. So I called Thornton Haggis to see if the Monument Works had any record, and he delved in the archives. No answer. So I went to the bank where my grandmother's diaries are kept in a large lockbox. That dear woman! I found out that Matilda was a cat! The relatives wouldn't object to burying an animal in the private cemetery, but they wouldn't want her to be called Matilda Campbell.

Anyway, here's the story, Qwill. Matilda was a gray mouser who went out every night and was always pregnant. That was normal.

But on one occasion she had catfits all day and all night. It was the night the little green lights appeared in the sky. We call them UFOs, but they called them "visitors". They weren't unfriendly— just interesting. They visited every seven years.

Sure enough, seven years later, Matilda went through the same performance! . . . But four years later, when she was fourteen—and pregnant again—she made another great fuss. My grandfather said, "I smell a tornado! We're going to a safe place!" He loaded the family and their valuables and the hunting dogs in the wagon, but Matilda was under the floor of the barn and wouldn't come out; they could hear her mewing. She was giving birth—again. The sky was turning black; they had to leave.

Good choice!—as they say nowadays. They returned to find the house wrecked. But the barn and Matilda and her four kittens were safe. When she died the next year, of natural causes, Grandmother insisted on burying her in the Campbell plot, among all the intrepid, illustrious Campbells.

25.

How Pleasant Street Got Its Name

Does the Name of a Street Affect Its Quality of Life?

Probably not, but pleasant people have been living in Carpenter Gothic houses on this very pleasant street for a century. Burgess Campbell, descendant of the original builder, tells the story behind the short cul-de-sac in Pickax.

—JMQ

In the nineteenth century my ancestors were shipbuilders in Scotland—in the famous river Clyde at Glasgow. When opportunity beckoned from the New World, my great-grandfather, Angus, came here with a team of ships' carpenters considered the best anywhere. They started a shipyard at Purple Point, where they built four-masted wooden schooners, using Moose County's hundred-and-twenty-foot pine trees as masts. These were the "tall ships" that brought goods and supplies to the settlers and shipped out cargoes of coal, lumber, and stone.

Then came the New Technology! The wireless

▼▼▼

telegraph was in; the Pony Express was out. Railroads and steamboats were in; four-masted schooners were out. In his diary Angus said it was like a knife in the heart to see a tall ship stripped down to make a barge for towing coal. There was no work for his carpenters to do, and their fine skills were wasted.

Then a "still small voice" told him to build houses! It was the voice of his wife, Anne, a canny Scotswoman. She said, "John, build houses as romantic as the tall ships—and as fine!"

She was right! The New Technology had produced a class of young upwardly mobile achievers who wanted the good life. Not for them the stodgy stone mansions built by conspicuously rich mining tycoons and lumber barons! They wanted something romantic!

So Angus bought acreage at the south edge of Pickax and built ten fine houses, each on one-acre plots. Although no two were alike, their massing followed the elongated vertical architecture called Gothic Revival, and the abundance of scroll trim was the last word in Carpenter Gothic.

And here is something not generally known:

▼▼▼

The vertical board-and-batten siding was painted in the colors that delighted young Victorians: honey, cocoa, rust, jade, or periwinkle; against this background, the white scroll trim had a lacy look.

Today we paint them all white, giving rise to the "wedding cake" sobriquet.

When the time came to put up signboards, Angus was at a loss for a street name. He said, "I don't want anything personal like Campbell or Glasgow . . . or anything sobersided or high-sounding . . . just something pleasant."

And Great-Grandma Anne said with sweet feminine logic, "Call it Pleasant Street."

▼▼▼

26.

The Noble Sons
of the Noose

Secret Society Goes Public
After a Hundred Years

Every year at midnight on May 13, a line of thirty-two shrouded figures—wearing miners' helmets with tiny lights above the visors—winds across the slag heaps of the abandoned Goodwinter mine—in memoriam.

—JMQ

On May 13, 1904, thirty-two miners were killed in an underground explosion that could have been prevented if the new safety measures had been employed; but they cost money, and the mine owner, Ephraim Goodwinter, was the original bottom-liner. Production was what counted. His mine was the most productive in the county, and he was the wealthiest owner.

Then, because there were no longer any males to work underground, their families were evicted from the poor cottages in the mining village. A murderous rage against Ephraim consumed the entire county, and the mine owner disappeared. Rumors abounded:

He had been lynched . . . Or he had taken his own life, leaving a suicide note . . . Or he had fled to Europe . . . Or he had been buried under the floor of his own house, to thwart vandals . . . Or he had escaped via a preplanned scheme arranged with the handyman, whom he then shot for security reasons.

One fact went on record: Ephraim's funeral procession was the longest ever—in a community fond of counting the carriages, buggies, wagons, and bicycles going to the cemetery (the undertaker later confessed, on his deathbed, that Ephraim's coffin was empty). The "mourners" said they wanted to be sure the "old devil" didn't come back.

The lynching party insisted on their claim, while maintaining anonymity, and so the secret society originated. The thirty-two silent figures still file across the slag heaps on May 13. In recent years, however, they have replaced "hating" with "helping". Many members are descended from families left fatherless by the explosion, and they

▼▼▼

volunteer as Saturday Dads for youngsters who have none. Their fraternal insignia of a hangman's noose has become the noble head of a bull moose!

One note in retrospect: The "old devil" tried to make amends by giving the county a large sum of money for a public library. It stands on Park Circle in Pickax, looking like a Greek temple. In the vestibule is an oil portrait of Ephraim Goodwinter. The canvas has been slashed—and poorly repaired.

▼▼▼

27.

Phineas Ford's Fabulous Collection

As Told by the Late Prentiss Campbell III

Believe this one at your own risk! Four generations of Campbells in Moose County have been known for their Scottish sense of humor. Burgess Campbell, a lecturer at Moose County Community College and son of Prentiss III, remembers it like this:

—JMQ

Back in the 1920s there was a feed-and-seed dealer in Brrr Township who was a real nice guy—hardworking, honest with his customers, and devoted to his wife. They had no children, and it was his way of showing kindness and understanding by taking her for a ride every Sunday afternoon in his Maxwell. Or was it a Model T? They would buy strawberries or a pumpkin, depending on the season, and stop at an ice-cream parlor in town for a soda.

His wife also liked to visit antique shops. She never bought anything—just looked. Every town had an antique shop and every farmhouse had a barnful of junk and a sign that read ANTIQUES. As she wandered through the jumble of castoffs, her husband trudged behind her, looking left and right and wondering why people bought such stuff.

Once in a while he played a little joke on her as they drove. She would say, "Stop! There's an antique shop!" And he would say, "Where? Where?" and speed up. Sometimes she'd insist that he turn around and go back.

On one of these occasions she had her own way, and they visited a farmhouse collection of this and that, Phineas traipsing dutifully behind his wife. Suddenly he saw something that aroused his curiosity, and he asked the farmwife what it was.

"A scamadiddle," she said. "Early American. Very rare. Found only in the Midwest."

"How much do you want for it?"

"Oh, a dollar, I guess," she said.

"Give you ninety cents." Phineas was no fool.

He carried it to the car and put it on the backseat, causing his wife to ask, "What's that thing?"

"What thing?"

"That thing on the backseat."

"That's a scamadiddle," he said casually, as if

▼▼▼

he bought one every day. "Early American, you know. Very rare. Found only in the Midwest."

"Oh," she said. "What are you going to do with it?"

"Put it in the china cabinet."

Every weekend after that, Phineas found pleasure in antiquing, forever searching for another scamadiddle. One Sunday he found it! Now he had two! He was a collector!

They began to travel farther afield, into adjoining counties, and to Phineas's delight there was an occasional scamadiddle to be found. The shopkeepers, knowing his interest, kept their eyes open and produced an occasional treasure. He was paying two dollars now—and no dickering. He built a room onto their house, lined with shelves and one glass case for choice examples.

The breakthrough came when another collector died, and Phineas bought his entire collection. A magazine called him the Scamadiddle King. He built another, larger room and paid the high dollar for the few remaining scamadiddles. Three museums were bidding to buy the Phineas Ford Collection posthumously.

▼▼▼

Then tragedy struck! One fateful night his house was struck by lightning and burned to the ground, reducing the entire scamadiddle collection to ashes.

And that's why—today—there's not a single scamadiddle to be found in the United States.

Coming in January 2004

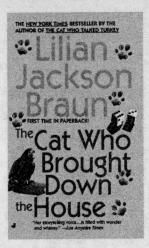

0-515-13655-7
First Time in Paperback

Actress Thelma Thackeray is organizing a
fundraiser revue starring Koko the cat. But
Thelma's celebration takes an unpleasant turn
when her brother is murdered and Jim Qwilleran
is the suspect. Can Koko put aside stardom
to lend a helping paw in the case?

B147

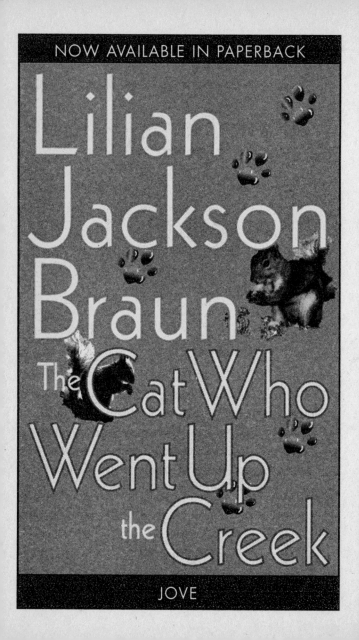

Lilian Jackson Braun

The Cat Who Went Up the Creek

JOVE